THORFINN THE NICEST VIKING

For Ross – D.M.

To Barney, the wildest of wild cats ever – R.M.

Young Kelpies is an imprint of Floris Books
First published in 2016 by Floris Books

Text © 2016 David MacPhail. Illustrations © 2016 Floris Books
David MacPhail and Richard Morgan have asserted their rights
under the Copyright, Designs and Patent Act 1988 to
be identified as the Author and Illustrator of this work

The publisher acknowledges subsidy from
Creative Scotland towards the publication
of this volume

MIX
Paper from
responsible sources
FSC
www.fsc.org   FSC® C007785

This book is also
available as an eBook

British Library CIP data available
ISBN 978-178250-229-6
Printed in Great Britain
by Bell & Bain Ltd

Thorfinn
and the
Rotten Scots

written by David MacPhail

illustrated by Richard Morgan

Young Kelpies

ERIK THE EAR-MASHER

VELDA

OLAF SON OF
ERIK THE EAR-MASHER

RANALD MACRANALD

CASTLE RED WOLF

THORFINN'S VOYAGE

NORWAY

SCOTLAND

CHAPTER 1

It was the Dark Age in Scotland, when men were big and hairy, and women were also big and hairy, and EVERYONE was scared of the Vikings.

Where the Highlands met the Lowlands, the mountains and forests gave way to rolling hills, farms – and lots of towns.

Rich towns. Just the kind of towns Vikings loved to plunder.

One day, a young Viking boy strolled out of the deep dark woods, a speckled pigeon perched on his shoulder. He walked up to the gates of the nearest town.

The guards on the walls bristled with weapons.

"Who goes there?" they growled.

A well-meaning grin spread across the boy's face. He took off his helmet and saluted them. "Good day, dear sirs. How pleased I am to meet you. My name is Thorfinn the Very-Very-Nice-Indeed. And this..." he stroked the bird's head, "...is my pigeon, Percy. We're calling today on behalf of the Vikings."

❋ ❋ ❋

Meanwhile, back in the woods, the rest of the Viking raiders waited.

And waited...

"RRR! Where is he?" cried Erik the Ear-Masher. He

had a giant beard, a face like a mangled turnip, and only one eye.

"You're always spoiling for a fight, aren't you?" roared Harald the Skull-Splitter, whose beard was bigger and bushier than Erik's, a sure sign he was the chief.

"We should never have sent your son to deliver terms," growled Erik. "Him and that daft bird."

Erik's son, Olaf, roared in agreement, "He never does it right." Olaf's face looked like a potato that had been forced through a mangle. "The Viking way!"

(The 'Viking way' just meant lopping someone's head off with a huge axe.)

"Hear, hear!" cried the men.

Olaf was on a roll now. "He's an embarrassment!

He makes friends wherever he goes. We Vikings HATE friends!"

"YEAAAHHHH!" cried the mob.

"DOWN WITH FRIENDS!" Olaf climbed up a nearby tree so everyone could see him. "Who needs 'em? We want enemies, not friends! Death to all friends!"

"YYYEEEEAAAHHHH!"

"Oh, except my pal Sven the Head-Crusher from the next village," said one of the men.

"Oh, yes, and Yorgar the Elk-Herder. He's a good laugh," said another.

"And Yoren the Monk-Slinger. He's good at wrestling."

"Alright! Alright! But why don't we just charge?" cried Olaf.

"Yesss!!" they all agreed.

Oswald, the village wise man and Thorfinn's friend, interrupted them: "SHUUSSH!" He had an incredibly loud and whiny voice. He sounded like a sheep with asthma. "Thorfinn might have a good reason for not coming back. "

"YEH!" Now Velda piped up. She was also Thorfinn's friend, a small girl with a very large helmet and an even larger axe. Girls weren't usually allowed on Viking voyages, but she had proved herself as one of the village's best axe throwers. "Don't forget, he has saved you many times. If it hadn't been for Thorfinn you'd all be elk fodder, the lot of you!"

"Rubbish!" cried Erik the Ear-Masher. "He's probably down there baking scones with them!"

"Yeah! Or drinking tea!" yelled Olaf.

16

"Yeah! Or playing scrabble!" added Erik.

"So what are we waiting for?" cried Olaf.

The Vikings were about to break cover and charge, when Harald himself erupted:

"SHUT UUUUUPPP!"

He whipped out his sword and sliced the nearest tree in half. "YAAAAHH!"

The tree crashed to the ground and the men leapt back in fear.

"We will give Thorfinn another hour. Then, if he's still not back, we charge. Is that clear?" demanded Harald.

17

* * *

Which is why, as dusk fell an hour later, a heavily armed band of Vikings stormed out of the woods to attack the town.

"Slaughter them!" they shouted.

"Make mincemeat of them!"

"Turn them into burgers!"

"Sausages!"

"Mash!"

"My tummy's rumbling."

"Did I mention I was hungry?"

"SHUT UP, you bunch of useless dogs!" cried Harald. "Let's show these lily-livered town-dwellers some of your Viking wrath!"

CHAPTER 2

"RAAAAARRR!" the Vikings yelled as they charged towards the town, then stopped dead in their tracks. The town gates were wide open and the streets were deserted.

"Where is everyone?" asked Erik the Ear-Masher.

The group wandered along the main street towards the sound of music, singing and dancing, which was coming from the town square.

A door burst open. Harald's men raised their swords, expecting a surprise attack, but it was just an old woman carrying a baby.

"Oh, there you are," she said, without the slightest hint of fear. "Thorfinn said you'd be coming."

"My son, Thorfinn?" asked Harald.

"Yes, such a lovely boy, and look, you've come dressed up as well. How lovely. Here, hold this..." She thrust the baby into Harald's arms. "Come on, lads." She led them over to a large table stacked with food. "Help yourselves!" The Vikings' eyes lit up as she handed out pieces of pie, slices of cake and wedges of cheese. Then she started doling out flagons of ale from a large barrel.

The men sheathed their weapons. They'd hardly eaten for three days, and they accepted the food and ale eagerly.

"Mmmm, nice cake," said one of them.

The baby smiled at Harald, and he found himself smiling back.

"Coochee-coochee-cooo!" he said, before he shook himself out of it and plonked the baby back into the woman's arms. "Wait, where's Thorfinn?"

"Follow me," she said, and led them down the street towards the music.

In the square, a large party was taking place. The townspeople were dressed in their finest clothes, and the buildings were festooned with flags and bunting. The tables were piled high with food, and there was more ale splashing about than the Vikings had ever seen.

Harald and his men felt slightly embarrassed as they trooped in, dirty, smelly and steaming with sweat, but to their surprise everyone cheered. People were slapping their backs and thrusting pie and ale into their already-full-of-pie-and-ale hands.

"Very good!" said the townspeople. "They're hilarious! Yes, very realistic!"

Harald's band stood in the midst of the applauding crowd. No Viking would admit it, but they were a tiny bit scared.

"No one we've attacked has cheered us before," said one of them.

"Don't they realise we're ruthless barbarians?" said Erik. "What's wrong with these people?"

Just then Harald caught sight of Thorfinn. He was sitting on a barrel at the very centre of the party, with his pigeon perched on his shoulder. The townspeople were listening to him eagerly.

"Go on, Thorfinn, tell us another of your braw riddles."

"Very well," said Thorfinn.

"I am lighter than what I am made of.
More of me is hidden than you can see.
I am the curse of the sailor.
What am I?"

The people clapped. "Very good, very good."

"Oh, that is an interesting one," said the wise man Oswald, hobbling up to join Thorfinn.

Velda was the only one who didn't seem impressed. "I hate riddles. They're boring. And too easy."

"So, what's the answer then, smarty pants?" asked Oswald.

Velda sighed. "Simple. What floaty things do we have to watch out for when we're sailing in the northern sea?"

Oswald cried out, "ICEBERGS!"

"Correct!" said Thorfinn, at which point Oswald broke into a kind of dance. Nowadays we would call it a moonwalk but no one had walked on the moon back then. Let's call it a cakewalk instead.

Harald barged through the crowd, glaring at his son.

"Father, dear, how pleased I am to see you," said Thorfinn. "I told my new friends here all about you and the others."

"Yes, we can see that," replied Harald. He had an incredibly twitchy eye when he got angry. Mostly it

25

twitched at his enemies, but now it was twitching at Thorfinn.

Harald turned to his men, only to find they had vanished. Some had been whisked off to dance with the townswomen. Others had joined a conga line, which was snaking its way round the square.

Even Erik and Olaf had wandered off to watch an arm-wrestling competition.

A short, podgy man stepped forward and grinned from ear to ear. "Ach, Mr Skull-Splitter, it's yerself! Thorfinn told us aw about ye."

Harald was about to whip out his sword and chop the man's head off, when the man grabbed his hand and began shaking it up and down.

"I'm the Mayor here. Ye know, when Thorfinn first turned up at oor gates we were terrified. We thought the real

Vikings had come tae burn doon our toon. Then he started talking... and aw, what a polite wee laddie. It was only then that we realised – you weren't the real Vikings at aw, just a friendly group of entertainers. Whit a great idea, though, pretending to be Vikings. I mean, we Scots, we love a good laugh better than anybody."

A steward walked past carrying a giant platter of roast goat. Harald caught a whiff and his stomach rumbled. It was without doubt his number one favourite meat in the world.

"Mmmm."

Harald shook the man's hand firmly.

CHAPTER 3

It wasn't until later...

Much later...

I mean MUCH, MUCH later...

After the Vikings had been fed and water and slept in comfy feather beds for the night. After a large breakfast of roast meats, honeyed gammon and glazed venison. After Harald had his portrait painted shaking hands with the Mayor...

In fact, it wasn't until they were marching up the hill away from the town, with their new friends lined

up on the walls shouting "BYE-EEE", that it finally hit Harald.

"What was all that about?" he cried, grabbing Thorfinn's shoulder.

"I thought it went swimmingly, Father. Oh, dear me, did I do anything wrong?" replied Thorfinn.

"Swimmingly?!" cried Erik the Ear-Masher, as Harald walked away with his head in his hands. "We should be up to our eyes in loot. Look at me!" Erik was wearing a garland round his neck and had roses in his hair. Some small girl had painted his fingernails pink while he was sleeping. "This is NOT what a Viking should look like."

Oswald jabbed Erik with his walking stick. "Thanks to Thorfinn, you all have full bellies, you've

slept in comfy beds and you drank an entire river's worth of ale."

"Bah!" Erik replied. "We can't have this milksop child and his pet bird going ahead of us at every town we hit. He's supposed to be a spy, not a party entertainer! "

"They thought we were a bunch of Viking impersonators!" said one man tearfully.

"We'll end up going back to Norway with nothing!" said another.

"Why do we always have to take him on our voyages?" asked Olaf.

Velda stood right in front of Erik and Olaf, her arms folded angrily, glaring up at them from under the lip of her helmet. "You know fine well why. Thorfinn is the cleverest of us all. We need him!"

Erik ignored her and appealed to his chief, Harald. "We came here to burn, loot and pillage, not to have our fingernails painted."

Thorfinn scratched his head. "I don't understand. Why would you want to come on holiday just to burn, loot and pillage?"

"How many times do we have to tell you? This is

NOT a holiday!" cried Erik. He tore off his garland, ripped the flowers out of his hair and started scrubbing away at his nails, except the pink varnish wouldn't come off. "BAHH!"

Harald took his second-in-command aside. They stood on top of one of the first foothills of the Highlands, looking down over rolling fields and a string of peaceful little towns stretching into the distance.

"Do you see that?" said Harald quietly. "There's rich plunder to be had in these Lowlands."

"Yes. But Thorfinn—"

"Leave my son to me. I have a plan to keep Thorfinn out of our way."

CHAPTER 4

The Vikings stopped at the next forest for a break. Thorfinn was busy feeding his pigeon. Harald knelt down on one knee beside him and placed his hand on his son's shoulder. "Now, then, Thorfinn. I have a special job for you."

"How wonderful! I do love the word 'special', don't you?"

"Yes..."

"Also the word 'blancmange'."

"Yes, OK..."

"And the word 'jamboree'. That's a jolly one, isn't it?"

"THORFINN!" Harald bit his lip before starting again in his slowest, calmest voice. "We will camp in these woods tonight. I want you, Velda and Oswald to go ahead and make a shelter for us. Do you understand?"

"Oh, goodie! I do love setting up camp. It's my favourite part of the holiday."

"It's NOT a holid—" Harald bit his lip even harder. He wondered, as he had many times, if his dear son was a few oars short of a longship. Why couldn't he have a normal Viking child, who liked burning stuff down and having burping competitions?

But Thorfinn was so eager, it was impossible to be angry with him for long.

"I'll do a great job, I promise. I'll find the perfect spot and we can tell cosy bedtime stories, and we'll need a stream for washing-up, and..."

His kind, well-meaning face was enough to melt the hardest of hearts, even a Viking chief's.

Harald sighed. "Yes, I know you'll do a good job. That's why I chose you." He lifted his son up in an enormous bear hug, before heading off after the other Vikings.

"He just wants to keep us out of the way while they do some proper Viking pillaging," Velda said quietly to Oswald. "It's not fair. Why don't I get to go off and do the fun stuff?"

"I'm quite happy. I can have
a nice sit down," said Oswald.
"My bunions are killing me."

As he joined the other
Vikings, Harald turned and
called back, "Don't worry if we're
not back for a while." He glanced at
Erik, who grinned. "We're off to... er... scout the area."

* * *

Velda sulked while Thorfinn whistled merrily on
their hunt for a good campsite. Percy took to the
air and followed them, swooping from branch to
branch.

"Oh, my bunions!" cried Oswald. "Take my mind

off them, Thorfinn. Tell me another one of your riddles."

"Oh, please no!" moaned Velda.

"Very well. Try this one," said Thorfinn.

"Two fathers and two sons are out hunting. They each catch one wood pigeon to take home. However, when they arrive they only have three wood pigeons.

How can this be?"

"Oh dear, that *is* a tough one," said Oswald, thinking.

"OK, I have one too," cried Velda. "*What's this sharp, bony thing at the end of my leg?*" She held up her foot, then swung it back as if she was about to let loose a massive kick. "*And how sore is it going to be when I boot you both up the backside?* Now let's stop wasting time and get on with our mission."

✱ ✱ ✱

At last, they found an excellent spot: flat and sheltered and near a river.

Velda went off to collect wood, while Thorfinn rushed to set up the camp. Oswald fell flat on his back and threw his arms out, shouting, "Ohh, my poor tootsies!"

Within half an hour Thorfinn had rigged up a large tent, made a fire and built a roasting spit, from which he hung a kettle.

They sat warming their feet by the fire and drinking tea. Percy flew down and perched on Thorfinn's shoulder.

"Ahh! What an excellent holiday this is," said Thorfinn.

"It is NOT a hol—" Velda began then sighed. "Oh, what's the point?"

Suddenly, their definitely-NOT-a-holiday was interrupted by a WHOOSH of air past their ears. An arrow embedded itself into a nearby tree:

THWOCK!

CHAPTER 5

Percy squawked and took to the air just as a group of fierce-looking men emerged from the bushes. They had long braided hair, thick beards, and wore reddish-coloured tartan kilts. One of them was pointing a bow and arrow at Thorfinn and his friends.

The man at the front was huge and muscly with a thick mane of red hair.

"I am Ranald MacRanald, chieftain of Clan MacRanald, otherwise known as The Red Wolf. Who are you?" he growled.

Oswald spoke first, jabbing a finger at the man with the bow. "You could have had my eye out with that thing, young man!"

"Fire another one at the auld codger!" said Ranald.

The bowman let loose a second arrow, which parted Oswald's hair.

"OHH, you're going to be sorry you did that," said Velda. "SOOO sorry." She whipped out her axe.

"Oh yes, little girl," said Ranald, knocking the axe from her hands with his huge sword. "And why's that?"

Velda stood her ground. "We're Vikings, and you don't mess with us."

"Vikings!" The men chattered excitedly. "Actual Vikings! We've captured real Vikings!"

"In fact, this boy is the son of our chief Harald the Skull-Splitter. You've probably heard of him."

There was more excited chatter among the clansmen:

"Oh aye, he's quite famous!"

"He's one of my favourites, he is!"

"We've captured the Skull-Splitter's son!"

Ranald turned to his men and rubbed his hands.

"See, I told you, we can be *at least* as tough as the Vikings. At least!"

Thorfinn stepped in front of Ranald and took off his helmet. "Now that we're all acquainted, could I offer you and your men a cup of tea?"

The Scots stared at Thorfinn's kettle like it was a rat sandwich.

"Tea?" said one of them. "Is that what Vikings drink?"

"Is that their secret? Does it make you tougher?" asked another.

"Should *we* be drinking tea?"

"Don't be daft! He's playing with us. Vikings don't drink tea," said Ranald. "I have a plan. We'll take them back to the castle and ransom them."

Two men grabbed Velda. She kicked, and screamed at them. "Oh, you're going to be SOOOO sorry! When Harald finds us, he'll chop you into little bits! He'll mince you and stick you in a curry!"

Thorfinn, on the other hand, was brimming with excitement as they dragged him away. "Oh, a castle! I love castles. Sadly most of the castles I see get burnt to the ground. I'd rather like to see one that wasn't."

"Wheesht!" cried Ranald. "Shooglin' numpties! You're prisoners; you're supposed to be quiet."

Ranald's men pushed their three captives into the forest while Percy followed overhead. They walked about fifty metres before Oswald started complaining about his feet again, then another fifty before he demanded to be carried.

Ranald sighed. "Silly old fool!" He prodded one of his men. "Winkie! Carry him!"

If anything, Winkie was even older, scrawnier and more decrepit than Oswald.

"Whit? I'm no' carrying him!" the man protested.

"Shuddup and get on with it!"

Winkie was a good name for this old fossil. He had a gurney, screwed-up face and blinkie eyes.

He staggered and gasped as Oswald leapt onto his back. "You're a ton weight, auld man!"

"Rubbish! I live on a diet of raw cabbage and apples." To make his point, Oswald let loose a colossal FART. "See?"

✳ ✳ ✳

They soon left the forest behind. The path carried them many miles over hills, moors and steep passes into the Highlands, before finally descending to a sea loch.

"There's Castle Red Wolf," said one of the Scots, pointing to a tumbledown fort perched on a rocky crag that jutted out into the water.

"Oh look, they have a beach," said Thorfinn. He turned to one of Ranald's men. "Do you have buckets and spades at the castle? How about deck chairs?"

The man just stared back at him, horrified.

By now Winkie was red-faced and wheezing, which did not add to his looks. "AHHHH! Ah need a rest!" he gasped.

Oswald whipped him with his cane. "Come on! Move!"

They followed the path down to Castle Red Wolf.

CHAPTER 6

As they neared the castle they realised what a terrible state it was in. Some of the walls had rotted away. Most of the windows were boarded over. Ranald's flag flew over the ramparts, a red wolf on a black background. The motto underneath read:

time to get tough

Judging by the giant holes in the roof, and the cacophany of cooing from within, many pigeons were living in the castle.

Thorfinn called up to Percy, "Oh, look, you'll

have loads of friends here." Percy seemed to nod, then flew up to the roof, where the other pigeons squawked to welcome him.

They trooped through the gate and into the castle courtyard. It was just as grimy here as it was outside. Armed men slouched around. The only activity came from the forge, where new swords and spears were being made.

Winkie threw Oswald off his back and then slumped to the ground, yelling, "Ah'm gonnie die!"

Oswald stood up, dusted himself down and sniffed. "Well, that was a most uncomfortable way to travel."

A group of women hanging around outside the entrance to the castle keep started jeering.

"Oh, here they come, our gallant menfolk!" cried

a large woman with rosy cheeks and red hair. A tartan shawl was draped over her shoulders. "What have you brought us this time? Food? Supplies? No, I didn't think so."

Ranald glared at the woman. "Even better, Maggie. We have brought Viking hostages. The son of a chief!"

"Big wow!" cried Maggie, who was in charge of running the castle. "And while you're busy wandering the countryside, kidnapping children and old folk, how are we supposed to tend our crops or repair the castle?"

Thorfinn turned to one of Ranald's men. "Excuse me, sir, but would you please tell me where the tennis courts are?"

The man looked insulted. "There are no tennis courts here, laddie."

"Oh, dear, that's a shame," said Thorfinn. "Then what other activities do you offer? Bowls? Croquet?"

Ranald's voice boomed out, "ENOUGH! Take the prisoners into the great hall."

✳ ✳ ✳

The great hall was stark and bare. The only furnishings were large tapestries showing bloody battle scenes. Some appeared to show members of the MacRanald clan defeating Vikings.

The three prisoners were thrown to their knees in front of the chieftain's throne. Ranald slumped down on it and studied Thorfinn, who was looking around the room with a well-meaning smile.

"Charming tapestries," said Thorfinn. "The weaver has really captured the spirit of battle."

"Enough of your tittle-tattle, laddie," Ranald fumed. "Now then, we're going to send a little ransom note off to your father. What do you have to say about that?"

"You won't get away with this, you good-for-nothing, lousy, rotten Scots—" Velda screamed before the guards pinned her down.

"By the way," said Thorfinn absent-mindedly, "do you by any chance have an indoor pool? It's just that my friend Oswald suffers from terrible bunions—"

"Still playing the fool, eh?" yelled Ranald.

"Oh, you have NO idea!" groaned Velda.

"Well, I tell you what, young Viking boy. I know what an insult it is for a Viking to be pampered! Tomorrow you will sit with the little children, the old men, the wounded and the weaklings and watch my men train in the practice yard." Ranald turned to Glen, his chief steward, a tall man with long grey hair and a sober face. "No weapons, no ale, not even watered-down. And give him the comfiest seat we have, the one we usually keep for the bishop."

"How kind," said Thorfinn.

"Ha! Putting on a brave face now," said Ranald. "But a bit of spoiling and we'll soon see you crack!"

The three captives were hauled to their feet and dragged upstairs, with Oswald whining, "Make sure I get a comfy seat too..." and Velda kicking and yelling. "The Vikings will chop you into chunks and feed you to the dogs..."

CHAPTER 7

Ranald went over to his desk, which he rarely used except for signing death warrants. "Now, we're going to write this ransom note. And because I want it to look really tough I'm going to write it in blood." He unfurled a scroll, picked up his dirk and turned to the nearest man he could find. "You!"

It was Winkie, who was still wheezing after carrying Oswald.

"Draw this blade across your palm, man," Ranald roared, "so I can use your blood."

"Whit...? Are you kiddin'?" replied Winkie.

"No, hurry up and do it!"

"B-but I've got the washing-up to do; it'll be really stingy!"

"In the name of Ben Nevis!" Ranald turned to his bowman. "You do it!"

"I can't!" replied the man. "I've got to fire arrows with this hand."

Ranald turned to his chief steward. "You do it, Glen."

Glen shook his head. "Alas, I cannot do it, my Lord."

"Why not!"

"It wouldn't be fitting for me to serve as your steward and greet guests with a bandaged hand."

"What guests? We never have any guests!"

"Well, you never know," shrugged Glen.

"We're supposed to be tough. Do you think the Vikings would be having this argument? They'd be queuing up to do it."

"Then why don't *you* do it, Chief?" said Glen.

"Why? Eh," Ranald smarted. "Well, I can't do it. I'm the chief."

"Excuse me," said Winkie, "but why do we no' just use something that *looks* like blood?"

"Like what?"

"We got loads of raspberries this summer. I could squash a handful oot and we could use the juice?"

"Raspberry juice? You want me to use raspberry juice?! It's meant to look tough. They'll think we're mad."

Ranald stared round at the blank faces of the men in the room, and his shoulders slumped. "OK then, we'll use raspberry juice."

✳ ✳ ✳

"This looks rubbish!" Ranald huffed as he finished his raspberry ransom note. "Oh, well, it'll have to do." He turned to the man nearest to him. "You!"

Yet again it was Winkie, who was by now on the verge of collapse. "I want you to march straight back over the hill and deliver this to the Viking chief."

Winkie nearly fainted. "Whit... me?!"

"Yes, you!"

"Why have ye always got tae pick on me?"

Ranald roared, his face the colour of a giant boil that was about to burst. "Don't argue with your chief! Just do it!"

Winkie snatched the message out of his chief's hands and hobbled slowly towards the door.

Ranald smothered his face in his hands. "Galloping galoots!"

✳ ✳ ✳

"Oh, you're going to be SOOOO sorry when the other Vikings get here," Velda cried as she, Thorfinn and Oswald were dragged along the corridor. "They're going to grind your bones to dust then use you as cat litter! They'll squish you into a paste then use you as pie filling!"

Thorfinn and Velda were thrown into a small, bare room, while Oswald got his own room next door.

Thorfinn got up, dusted himself off and looked around. The room was empty apart from two small beds and a tiny glassless window looking out onto the loch.

"Well, the accommodation is basic, but it does have air conditioning at least." He turned to the toilet recess: a plain stone seat and a hole with an icy draught blowing through it. "En-suite too!"

Velda threw herself on the hard woorden bed and folded her arms. "I'm going to escape. This castle won't hold me."

Thorfinn wasn't listening. He had stepped up to the window, his hands on his hips, and was gleefully looking out at the view. "And the scenery is just wonderful."

Velda rolled her eyes. "Besides, sharing with you will drive me round the twist."

CHAPTER 8

Velda barely slept that night. She was racking her brain trying to think up escape plans. Thorfinn on the other hand snoozed happily until morning, when they were woken abruptly and marched down to the great hall.

Breakfast was being served – if you could call it breakfast. It was porridge, which both looked and tasted like horse sick. Velda pushed her plate away but Thorfinn tucked his napkin under his chin and sampled it like it was some kind of exotic foreign cuisine.

Oswald started banging his fist on the table, shouting, "Don't you have any kippers? We want kippers!"

After this, the three captives were led down to the parade ground, where the MacRanald swordsmen were training. One of the guards grinned as he showed Thorfinn to his seat, on which a padded velvet cushion was placed. "Chieftain MacRanald is out hunting, but he has instructed me to guard you. Sit there, boy."

Thorfinn's eyes brightened. "Thank you so much. I feel very safe. And I could do with a nice sit down."

"I bet you could, little Viking boy!" the guard said in a mocking posh voice.

"You can't treat a Viking chief's son like this!" said Velda. "It's not right!"

This only fired the guards up. Now they cackled and taunted Thorfinn. "How about a nice little cup of tea and a biccie-wiccie while you watch the big strong men train?"

But Thorfinn didn't break as they'd hoped. In fact his face lit up. "Why, that would be just wonderful, thank you." The men could only scratch their heads.

It was Velda who was close to breaking point. "Please!" she cried, grabbing one of them round the ankles. "Throw me in the dungeon! Put me in chains! Just don't make me sit on that nice comfy seat!"

The only other people sitting there were two sad-looking old men.

"I'm Jock," said one of them as they sat down.

"And I'm Haggis," said the other.

"What? That's really your name? Haggis?" Oswald couldn't believe it. He burst out laughing, sounding like a giant parrot that had just been doused in itching powder.

"We're the wise men of the castle," said Jock.

"Aye, nobody listens to us," sighed Haggis.

Oswald rubbed his chin. "Well, seeing as you are wise men perhaps you can help me solve a riddle."

"Oh, we love riddles," said Jock, punching his hand.

"Aaaagh! Not riddles again!" cried Velda, clutching at her helmet and pulling it down over her ears. "I'd rather be boiled alive."

Oswald explained the riddle of the two fathers, two sons and three birds.

"Hmm, that is a tricky one," said Haggis.

"Do you give up?" asked Velda. "I'll tell you the answer—"

"Belt up, you lot!" cried one of the guards. "Prisoners are supposed to be quiet!"

"Oh, stuff this! I'm not sitting here any longer."

Velda leapt from her seat and charged towards the training men, shouting, **"VIKINGS FOREVER!"**

Then she went on the rampage, kicking men in the shins, pushing them into the mud, tweaking their noses, and somersaulting out of their grasp when they tried to stop her. Within seconds she'd turned Ranald's training session into a riot.

"She certainly knows how to liven up any occasion," said Thorfinn.

CHAPTER 9

Later that day, Ranald returned from the hunt, riding into the courtyard with a look of wicked glee across his face. His horse was festooned with deer, rabbits and partridges.

He dismounted and passed the reins to his chief steward, Glen.

"Well, how did the Viking boy fare watching the men practise? Did he crack? Did he break? Did he sob with jealousy?"

The steward was stony faced as he replied, "No, my Lord. In fact, he was heard to enjoy it."

Ranald's smile melted away. "WHAT??"

"I'm afraid so, my Lord."

"Did you give him the comfy seat?"

"Yes, he declared he was very happy with it."

Ranald's eyes blazed. "I'll show him. I will go and see this boy."

He stormed up the stairs to the corridor where the prisoners were kept. "Where is he?"

"SSSSHH!" said one of the stewards. Ranald suddenly realised that everyone in the corridor was tiptoeing.

"What is the meaning of this?" he asked.

"Because of the old man!"

Suddenly an incredibly loud and whiny voice cried out:

"QUUII-ETTTT!"

It sounded like the mating call of a Pacific albatross.

Oswald's head popped out from behind his door. "I'm trying to think, you know."

"Why is this man's door unlocked?" cried Ranald.

"It was just easier, sire. He kept banging on it and demanding things," said Glen.

"Things? What kind of things?"

Glen pulled a piece of paper from his tunic and opened it out, which took a moment because it was very long. "Ahem... a beard comb, a neck pillow, a foot muff, toenail clippers..."

"Aye, alright! Alright!" roared Ranald.

71

"It was just constant. My stewards were rushed off their feet," Glen explained.

Oswald came out of his room carrying a huge pile of dirty linen. "You there!" he cried at Ranald. "Stop loafing around and take my laundry!" He dumped the linen into Ranald's arms.

Ranald almost nodded and turned away before catching himself. "Wait! I'm The Red Wolf! I don't do laundry!" He angrily dumped the linen in a heap and stomped over to Thorfinn's room.

Thorfinn was already standing at the door with his usual good-natured smile.

"Playing a game, eh!" cried

Ranald, who was now red-faced with anger. "Well, I know the game you're playing. You think you're tougher than us, eh? You think you can't be cracked?"

Thorfinn interrupted him, gently raising his helmet. "Excuse me, sir, I'd just like to thank you and all the staff for your hard work."

"WHA—?!"

"Yes, it's been a wonderful stay so far, although I do have some feedback. You might want to advertise for a new janitor. I've noticed the building is in some disrepair."

Ranald shook his fist at him. "Disrepair? I'll show you disrepair." He stomped away in the direction of the great hall, yelling at the top of his voice. "He thinks he can toy with me? MEEEEE?!"

"Why don't you have a lie down, Chief?" said Glen, who followed close behind.

But Ranald wasn't listening. "If he wants to carry on this act let's up the stakes." He rubbed his chin as he thought of a plan. "Here's what we'll do. Tonight, give him a nice feather bed, the one reserved for royal visits. Give him fluffy slippers and a hot-water bottle. Any true Viking would be ashamed. And, since he's going on about the state of my castle, tomorrow you can put him and his friends to work cleaning it. Yes, servants' work: a major insult to any proud warrior. Besides, Vikings don't believe in cleaning." He laughed and slapped his hands together. "We'll see who cracks first!"

CHAPTER 10

Meanwhile, back in the Scottish Lowlands, Harald, Erik and the other Vikings were having a tremendous time laying siege to a small town.

"READY THE CABBAGES!" cried Harald. The Vikings loaded cabbages onto giant slings and waited for his command.

"FIIIIRE!!"

They launched wave after wave of cabbages over the town walls. Having vegetables catapulted at you was one of the worst insults imaginable for any Viking.

But Harald was puzzled. "I don't understand why they haven't surrendered yet. They should be dying of shame by now."

It was Olaf who put his hand up. "Excuse me, Chief, but maybe it's because we are firing food at them. Some people eat cabbages you know."

"Don't be ridiculous!" cried Harald. "Only a raving lunatic would eat vegetables or Oswald, and you know how he smells." Then he stroked his beard for a moment. "Thorfinn would know what to do," he

whispered to himself. "I wonder how he is...
I hope he found a comfy spot to pitch his tent..." He
told the others, "I need to go and have a think, lads."

As soon as he said this, the other Vikings dashed
for cover. Whenever Harald had to think, he threw axes
at trees. He was a rotten aim, so finding a safe place to
hide was a wise move. Some even dug trenches.

Harald wandered off into the woods while Erik the Ear-Masher and the other Vikings took cover and consulted the map. Just then, one of the Viking look-outs appeared.

"A messenger has arrived, looking for the chief."

Harald's axe could be heard from the woods thumping into a tree:

"I'll talk to him," said Erik.

Up toddled a very old man, panting with exhaustion and carrying a scroll. "My name is... Winkie of Castle Red Wolf, and I come... hot foot from my master's castle."

The Vikings burst out laughing. "YOU? Look at the state of you! You couldn't hot foot it if you were running from a stampeding elephant."

Winkie looked insulted, and Erik snatched the scroll from his hand. He read the message, mumbling: "To the Viking chief... your son, Thorfinn... have taken him hostage... ransom... toughest clan in Scotland... Castle Red Wolf... blah, blah, blah..." Erik stopped and sniffed the air. "Does anyone smell raspberries?"

"Well, Sir Viking, whit's your reply?" asked Winkie.

Another axe bounced from tree to tree before knocking out a passing stag:

BASH, BONK, THWANG!

"MY reply? Ha!" Erik laughed, a great booming

laugh that seemed to shake the ground and rattle everyone's chests. "I'll give you MY reply."

He tore off a piece of paper, scribbled on it, and handed it back to Winkie. "Now get going, before we tie you to a tree and use you as target practice!"

Winkie eyed a giant platter of roast chicken the Vikings had pillaged for lunch. "Oh, can I no' have a wee sit doon and a bite tae eat before I go?" he asked. "It's an awful long way back."

"No, I've got a better idea," replied Erik. "Drag him outside!"

The Vikings hauled the old man out of the tent, strapped him to a horse and slapped the horse on the hindquarters. The horse reared up and galloped off in the direction of the Highlands.

"H-HELLLLPPP!" Winkie wailed.

The Vikings roared with laughter, until an axe came hurtling out of the woods, whizzed passed their ears and landed in a tree trunk.

THHWWWUMMMP!

It was Olaf who broke the silence, turning to his father. "Dad, shouldn't we have told Harald the chief about Thorfinn before you sent back that message?"

"But why? This is our chance to get rid of Thorfinn once and for all," Erik replied.

CHAPTER 11

That night Thorfinn snuggled up in his comfy feather bed, complete with slippers, water bottle and hot chocolate. "Well, I must say, the service here is excellent."

But Velda wasn't listening. She was smearing charcoal over her face, commando-style. "SSSH, now come on Thorfinn, get out of bed. We're escaping!" She hauled him towards the door.

"I think you'll find the door is locked," said Thorfinn.

"Ha! There's no lock a smart Viking girl like me can't pick." She brandished a small pin and began probing the lock. Seconds later she flung the door wide open.

Next she unlocked Oswald's door. Oswald was pacing about the floor. "Ah, Thorfinn. I'm still trying to figure out your riddle. Let's see: two fathers, two sons..."

"Never mind that rubbish now," said Velda in hushed tones. "Follow me, and be quiet!"

She led Oswald and Thorfinn downstairs, halting in the shadows at the entrance to the courtyard while the guards passed by. "I've timed the sentries. They are about to swap shifts. This is our chance, but we only have a minute. Do you understand?"

They nodded.

Velda shoved her two friends into the courtyard. "Quick! Now!"

They skirted the wall, dodging between moonlight shadows.

"This is fun, isn't it?" said Thorfinn. "Are we off to raid the kitchens? We could have a midnight feast."

Velda pushed them towards a giant catapult. "Get on there." Thorfinn and Oswald squeezed themselves into the giant spoon-head where the missiles normally sat. "I've set it as high as it can possibly go." Velda squashed herself in behind them, then whipped out a knife and cut the cord.

PYOINNGGG!

"WHHHEEEEEEEEEEEEE!"

cried Thorfinn. Oswald cried out too. He sounded like a seagull having a panic attack.

They landed in a confused mess. When they got to their feet and dusted themselves off they were standing not on the ground outside, but on the highest battlements of the castle.

"Odin's beard!!" cried Velda. "We were too heavy

to get over the wall! Never mind, look there's a rope ladder we can use. We'll climb down the other side."

Velda heaved the bundle of ropes over the wall. She stretched her leg over and reached for Thorfinn's hand. "Come on!"

But Thorfinn wasn't paying attention. He was too busy taking in the beautiful view over the moonlit loch. "What a wonderful place you've brought us to. Stunning scenery." At that moment Percy flew down from the rooftop and perched on his hand. "Good evening, old pal," Thorfinn said as he lovingly stroked the bird's head. "This night just gets better and better."

"Grrr!" Velda turned and reached for Oswald instead. "Come on!"

Oswald made a strange clucking sound like a surprised chicken. "You must be joking! Climbing down there – with *my* feet!"

Velda yelled with frustration, just as a guard rounded the corner.

"Hey you lot!" he cried.

They'd been caught.

CHAPTER 12

The following morning Thorfinn's breakfast was served on a pewter tray scattered with rose petals. He had boiled eggs and buttered toast cut into soldiers.

"This place just keeps getting better and better," he said. But Velda was outraged. She screamed like a Valkyrie, jumped on the poor steward's back and pulled his head back by the nose.

"How DARE you serve such a breakfast to a Viking? We crush rose petals underfoot! And the only soldiers we eat for breakfast are real ones!"

It took a gang of Ranald's men to pull her off.

Afterwards, the three prisoners were given mops and buckets and led to the top of the castle. "You've to start at the top and work your way down," they were told.

Velda yelled after the guards as they left, "Oh, you're going to be SOOOO sorry when the other Vikings come for us. They're going to squash you into jelly and serve you with ice cream. They're going to play marbles with your eyeballs, rounders with your kneecaps, football with your skulls. Oh yeah! They'll churn you to a pulp! Then squirt you down a drain!"

Thorfinn smiled at his two friends and got to work. He put his heart and soul into it, whistling happily as he mopped his way down the corridor. "Well, this is fun, isn't it?" he said cheerily.

"No, it's not, Thorfinn. This is no job for a Viking," said Velda. "Is it, Oswald?"

But Oswald wasn't listening, he was still deep in thought. "Two fathers, two sons, three birds. How? Hmmm..."

Velda growled and broke her mop over her knee. And then, for good measure, she broke Oswald's as well.

"I'm off to the roof to figure out a new escape plan." She grabbed a coil of rope that was hanging from a rack and disappeared up a flight of steps.

"Well, I no longer have a mop, so I may as well have a rest," said Oswald, and he slumped down on the steps and immediately fell fast asleep.

"What a funny lot my friends are," said Thorfinn, and he turned back to mopping the floor.

When Ranald returned to the castle after a busy day terrorising the local peasants, he noticed something alarming. The castle was no longer flying his red-wolf banner from the great tower. In its place was what looked like a white flag, a flag of surrender.

"Jings! What on earth has happened? Have we been invaded?"

He galloped into the courtyard, jumped off his horse and drew his sword. "What's going on? There will be no surrender at Castle Red Wolf!"

But everyone in the courtyard was going about their business as normal. Glen looked at him with surprise. "Is something the matter, sire?"

Ranald jabbed his sword at the flagpole. "What's the idea, flying a white flag?"

"Oh, that," said Glen. "Don't worry, that's not a white flag."

Ranald sheathed his sword. "Then what is it?"

"It's the old man's underpants."

Ranald croaked. "WHAT?!"

"He's been hanging his laundry up all over the battlements. Said they needed airing."

"How dare he?! How dare *you*?! Take them down immediately!"

"Yes, Chief," Glen bowed, then turned to one of his stewards. "You there, take down the old man's underpants."

The steward gulped. Then Oswald himself leaned out of a window on the first floor, shaking his fist.

"Oi! Keep your HANDS OFF MY UNDERPANTS!"

CHAPTER 13

Once Oswald's pants had dried and the old wise man had taken them down, Ranald remembered about Thorfinn.

"How did the Viking boy fare with the cleaning?" he asked Glen. "Did he blub, did he whimper, did he bend?"

"No, I'm afraid not."

"WHATTT?!"

"In fact he cleaned the whole castle from top to bottom. He also fixed the leaky roof."

Ranald forgot himself for a moment. "Oh, the leaky

roof, that's good. It was right outside my chamber door. Drip, drip, drip – all night ..." Then he caught himself. "Oh, wait, no! What do you mean he fixed the roof?!"

"And he fixed the drains too. That awful cabbagey smell in the corridor is gone."

"I don't believe it."

"He also installed a belly-button-fluff collector in the bath house."

"SHUDDUP!" cried Ranald angrily.

"It's very good, actually. I tried it," said Glen.

"SHUDDUP! SHUDDUP!" Ranald's face had gone bright purple.

Glen pulled a scroll of paper from his tunic. "By the way, Winkie returned with the Vikings' reply to your ransom note."

"A-ha! At last some good news. This is what I've been waiting for."

Ranald snatched it from his steward, unrolled it and read the message inside.

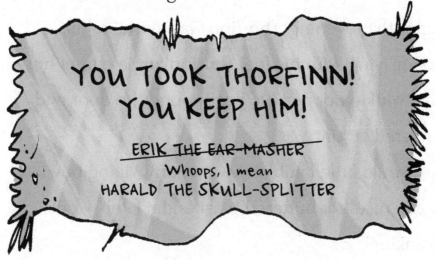

YOU TOOK THORFINN!
YOU KEEP HIM!

~~ERIK THE EAR-MASHER~~
Whoops, I mean
HARALD THE SKULL-SPLITTER

Ranald roared and tore the paper to pieces. "*They're* playing mind games too. But I'm smarter than them. Thorfinn will crack soon. Tomorrow he will be forced to sew and weave – the ultimate

insult for any Viking warrior. We'll break him once
and for all."

✳ ✳ ✳

Later that evening, Thorfinn was alone in his
room, lying with his feet up, drinking a cup of hot
tea. Winkie popped his head round the door and
sneered at him.

"Would little lambkiny-wambkiny Viking boy like
some nice hot buttered toast and a lambswool
blankie?"

Thorfinn's eyes lit up. "How thoughtful."

Winkie scowled, then slammed the door shut and
locked it. He hadn't noticed Velda was missing, her
place taken by a pillow hidden under a blanket.

A moment later, Percy appeared at Thorfinn's window, flapping his wings. "Oh, hello, old pal," said Thorfinn.

Percy took off again, fluttering about in the air excitedly.

"What's the matter? Do you want me to follow you?"

"Coo coo!" replied Percy and he flapped his wings faster.

"Well, lead on."

Thorfinn put his helmet on, then picked the lock, just like Velda had shown him. He crept down the corridor. At the end he found another window. A rope was hanging out of it, tied to the leg of a heavy oak table, which was wedged in the window frame.

"HELP!" came Velda's voice from somewhere beyond the window. With Percy fluttering about his ears, Thorfinn leaned out to see Velda dangling from the other end of the rope about twenty feet off the ground.

Thorfinn raised his helmet. "Good evening, my dear friend, but isn't it a bit late for abseiling?"

"Quit jabbering and pull me up!" Velda replied in a whisper. She was hanging outside the largest window of the great hall, where Ranald and his men were feasting.

"No problem, old friend," said Thorfinn.

"Hurry!" she said through gritted teeth. She was trying not to move, hoping they wouldn't spot her in the flickering light from their fire.

As Thorfinn began to pull, Winkie strolled over to the window. He peered out at Velda. Velda leaned forward and put on the scariest face she could. Winkie screamed.

"There's a monster at the windie!"

Thorfinn gave one almighty heave and Velda flew up and onto the window ledge. Winkie turned back... and the monster was gone.

"Ha! No more ale for you," said Ranald.

"PHEW!" said Velda as she climbed back inside. "Foiled again! The pesky rope was too short! This castle is proving really hard to escape from!"

CHAPTER 14

The next morning, Velda was awoken by Winkie yelling in her ear, "HE'S GONE!"

She tumbled out of bed. Winkie was staring in horror at Thorfinn's empty bedcovers. He glared at her with his blinkie eyes. "Where's the Viking boy?"

She was just as surprised as he was. "I dunno."

Winkie cried out, "Sound the alarm. Thorfinn has escaped!"

Horns blared, hounds barked, men shouted. Then Ranald appeared, a look of smug satisfaction on his face.

"I knew he'd break somehow. Now he's done a runner, it gives us the chance to hunt him down!" He turned to his men: "Unleash the dogs of war!"

✳ ✳ ✳

In the courtyard, the hounds were baying for blood, and the horses strained at the leash as the search party mounted them. "After him!" cried Ranald.

"YYAHHH!" cried his men, and they charged out of the castle gate.

Shadowed closely by a guard, Velda followed them out to the drawbridge. It was only then, as Ranald and his men disappeared over the horizon in a cloud of dust, that Velda spotted Thorfinn.

He was sitting by the brook nearby, legs paddling in the water and a makeshift fishing rod in his hand. He was whistling and Percy was perched on his shoulder, cooing.

Velda ran over to him, while her nervous young guard drew his sword and called for reinforcements. "Thorfinn!" she said.

Thorfinn broke off his whistling, raised his helmet and smiled. "Good morning to you, dear friend. And to you, Mr Guardsman."

"What do you think you're doing?" said Velda.

"I hate to cause you any embarrassment, but isn't it a bit obvious?" He held up the fishing rod. He'd already caught a couple of trout, which were lying next to him on the grass.

The guard held his trembling sword out at Thorfinn. "D-D-Don't move!"

Thorfinn leaned forward and spoke quietly, "I don't intend to. Movement might scare off the fish."

"I don't get it," said Velda.

"I thought we might have something other than red meat on the menu tonight. It's bad for our arteries."

"I mean, how on earth did you escape?"

"Escape?" said Thorfinn, puzzled. "I just walked out the gate."

Velda clutched her head with her hands. "I don't believe it! I've been struggling to escape for days, and you just walk out the front door?"

"Yes," said Thorfinn. "The nice man at the gate was sleeping and I didn't want to wake him so early."

More guards arrived and drew their swords.

"Watch him, he's tricky!" said one.

"Get back inside now!" demanded another.

Thorfinn stood up. "Why, I'd be delighted to."

They marched him back into the castle in front of a forest of sword points, and took him straight to a large room, where some women were spinning wool and sewing. As they looked up, Thorfinn removed his helmet and bowed. "Good day, dear ladies. I'm delighted to meet you."

The women smiled. "What a pleasant wee laddie.

Come and join us!"

Thorfinn sat down, looking at their sewing patterns with interest. "Pardon me, but would you mind if I had a go?"

Maggie, the head seamstress, handed Thorfinn a needle and thread.

After a huge battle, the guards finally pushed Velda into the room. She looked around in horror at everyone sewing, then screamed:

"NOOOO!"

CHAPTER 15

It was late afternoon before Ranald and his men returned from their hunt, weary, sunburnt and downcast. Glen had the job of giving Ranald the bad news. Ranald's face took on the look of a bulging volcano.

"WHHHHAAAAATTTTT? You mean we've been coursing all over the hills and dales, scouring riverbeds, chasing through forests, and all the time he was RIGHT HERE?"

"I'm afraid so, sire."

Ranald roared with anger. "And did you make him

sew like I told you?"

"Yes, as instructed, sire."

"AND?" he demanded angrily. "Did he squeal? Crumble? Beg? Even a little bit??"

"I'm afraid not. In fact, he seemed to enjoy it."

"WHHHAAAATTT?!!" Ranald choked, his voice so high that some of the dogs started barking.

"In fact he taught the others some new sewing techniques. He's now giving a sewing class each evening at seven. He also spruced up the castle menu. We're having something called frittata tonight. And he helped the cook pass her hygiene certificate."

Ranald dropped to his knees and glared up at the sky, shaking his fists.

"ARRRRRRGGHH!"

When he got up, there was a determined look on his face. He drew his sword. "I have had it with this Viking boy. I'm going to deal with him once and for all. Where is he?"

✳ ✳ ✳

Harald the Skull-Splitter and his men were hiding in the rocks that overlooked Castle Red Wolf.

Erik the Ear-Masher stood at Harald's side, looking red-faced and sheepish. His hands were tied and there was a gag in his mouth. When Harald found out Thorfinn had been kidnapped, he'd soon uncovered Erik's trick. Harald glared at Erik. He still hadn't forgiven him for sending back the message telling the Scots to keep Thorfinn.

"I hope, for your sake, my boy is safe and well," he said as he peered closely at the battlements.

Erik could only cough in response.

Soon Harald spied a weakness in the castle's defences. "The sentry is looking the other way. Something must be distracting him, something from inside the castle... " He turned to his men. "Now's our chance. You boys ready?"

The Vikings had their swords drawn, war paint smeared across their faces, and coils of rope and grappling hooks at the ready. The gleeful look on their faces said it all.

"Ready, boss!"

"Let's bash those rotten Scots!"

"RAAAAAAR!"

Harald turned to Erik. "OK, I've punished you enough, Ear-Masher."

He slashed Erik's bonds and removed the gag.

Erik simply grunted and grabbed an axe.

Harald raised his sword over his head.

"Vikings, CHAAAAAAARGGGGE!"

CHAPTER 16

Meanwhile, Glen had taken Ranald to the practice yard, where practically everyone in the entire castle seemed to have gathered.

"What in the name of NESSIE'S BREEKS is going on here?"

Thorfinn was at the centre of the crowd sitting on a barrel. The castle wise men, Jock and Haggis, were propped up next to him. Everyone was listening intently.

Everyone, that is, apart from Velda, who was leaning against a wall with her arms folded.

"Go on, Thorfinn! Tell us another riddle," the crowd urged him.

"Very well," said Thorfinn:

"How far can a hound run into the woods?"

Oswald scratched his beard. "Hmm, now, it would depend on the wood, wouldn't it?"

"Yes," agreed Jock.

"Which wood is the hound running into?" asked Haggis.

"Ugh," said Velda, rolling her eyes. "The answer's *halfway*. It's always *halfway*."

"Very good," replied Thorfinn. "It doesn't matter what size the wood is, for once the hound is halfway through, if he keeps running he'll be going *out of* the wood again."

"Ah, very good, Thorfinn," cried Oswald, who started a round of applause.

At that point Ranald barged through the crowd with his sword drawn. He was seething with anger as he thrust his sword point at Thorfinn. "I have had it, boy! I'm going to run you through!"

He hoisted his sword over his head, ready to strike.

Maggie jumped in front of Ranald just in the nick of time.

"Oh no you don't!" Maggie yelled.

"WHATT?! What's the meaning of this?" cried Ranald, still holding his sword aloft.

"We're sick of you," replied Maggie. "You're horrible and mean all the time."

Ranald turned to his men. "Are you listening to this?"

But the men just shrugged. "My missus isn't happy," said one.

"They told us we were all useless, filthy oafs," said another. "And they're right: all we do is rampage about the countryside pretending to be as tough as Vikings."

"I wish you men were more like Thorfinn," said one of the women.

"Such a charming gentleman," agreed another.

Ranald practically had steam coming out of his ears. "You're AGREEING with them?" he asked the men.

"We don't want to be tough any more. We want to settle down and farm our crops," said one man.

"Yes, let's get this castle fixed up; it's an embarrassment," said Glen.

"Aye!" added Winkie. "And I'm fed up of you ordering me about aw the time—"

"ATTAAACK!" came another voice – a great booming one that Thorfinn recognised.

They turned to see Harald the Skull-Splitter standing on the battlements at the head of a heavily armed and seriously annoyed Viking band. The Vikings dropped to the ground from their ropes and surrounded the Scots.

"DAD!" cried Thorfinn, and he jumped into his father's arms. Harald lifted him up in a huge hug.

"Are you alright, Thorfinn?"

"Alright?" said Thorfinn. "Of course I am. I'm having a wonderful time."

Harald sighed with relief and put his son down. Then he turned to the MacRanalds and deployed his twitchy eye at them. Every man among them trembled. And they trembled a bit more when he lunged towards them.

"Now, what's all this?" he yelled. "We go to all the trouble of launching a brilliant and daring surprise attack on your castle, only to find no one's even watching! And you're all down here listening to my son telling riddles!"

Ranald fell to his knees and his face crumbled. He blurted out, "Thank heavens you've come!"

"Eh?" The Vikings were a bit taken aback by this. They were still expecting a big fight, despite the easy start.

"I know you said in your note that I should keep Thorfinn," said Ranald.

Harald shot a murderous look at Erik the Ear-Masher and his son, Olaf, who both shrank back out of sight.

"But, please, PLEASE..." Ranald clasped his hands together. "You've GOT to take him back. I can't stand it any more. I can't! I surrender!"

With that, Ranald collapsed on the ground, sobbing like a baby.

Thorfinn stepped forward. "I'm terribly sorry, but my father has come for me, so I'd better be going now."

He bowed at the Scots around him. "Thanks ever so much for having me."

"It's been our pleasure, Thorfinn," said Maggie.

Thorfinn turned away, but he stopped to take off his helmet to Ranald, who looked up at him, his face streaked with tears.

"I'd like to thank you, Mr MacRanald, and all the staff. It's been a wonderful holiday. I'll try and come back next year."

"WHAT? NOOOOOOO! Please! Go somewhere else! I hear England is lovely this time of year."

"Call yourself The Red Wolf? Red Wimp more like," said Velda, giving him a short, sharp kick in the ribs.

Harald shrugged and shook his head. "Let's go home."

Oswald slowly got to his feet, cradling his back, and glared at the Vikings. "Ooh, my bunions are the size of fruit scones. Who's going to carry me?"

CHAPTER 17

On the way back to their longship, Harald confided in Thorfinn. "You defeated that tough old dog Ranald with kindness, Thorfinn. Don't tell the others I said this, but even I know that sometimes *it's better to be nice.*" He whispered the last bit.

"I find it's *always* better to be nice, Father," replied Thorfinn.

Oswald jumped in the air. "That's it! I have the answer, Thorfinn. Two fathers and two sons in the wood, each bag a woodpigeon, but they only have three when they get home. The answer is there are only three men: a grandfather, a father and a son – which makes two fathers and two sons!"

Thorfinn beamed and shook the wise man's hand. "Well done, old friend. You finally got it."

Oswald began another elderly cakewalk. "At last!"

"It only took you a week," said Velda.

"Here's another one for you," said Thorfinn. "A man rides into an inn on Friday. He stays two nights, then he rides out again on Saturday. How can this be?"

Oswald groaned. "Oh no, that's a hard one!"

"I think I'll go and chuck myself in the sea," said Velda.

Thorfinn laughed and stroked Percy, and Percy cooed back at him.

"Goodbye Scotland! Break out the ale!" cried Harald as they turned to the east, away from the setting sun. "Or, in Thorfinn's case, the tea!"

"HUZZAH!" cried the crew as they sailed back towards Norway.

THE END

P.S. *The horse was called Friday.*

RICHARD THE PICTURE-CONQUEROR

DAVID THE STORY-CHIEF

DAVID MACPHAIL left home at eighteen to travel the world and have adventures. After working as a chicken wrangler, a ghost-tour guide and a waiter on a tropical island, he now has the sensible job of writing about yetis and Vikings. At home in Perthshire, Scotland, he exists on a diet of cream buns and zombie movies.

RICHARD MORGAN was born and raised by goblins on the Yorkshire moors. After running away to New Zealand to play with yachts and paint backgrounds for Disney TV he returned to the UK to write and illustrate children's books. He now lives in Cambridge, England, and has a family of goblins of his own.

A TIMELINE OF THE VIKINGS IN SCOTLAND – A SEASIDE SAGA*

795 AD When the Vikings first landed in Scotland, on the island of Iona, they claimed they were just looking for an ice-cream shop. But it was a trick! They locked the monks in the cellar, ransacked the monastery and nicked all their gold.

840 AD The Picts were the original people of Scotland and the Scots came across the sea from Ireland. The two tribes were always fighting – until the Vikings arrived, when they teamed up to fight the hairy invaders and formed the new kingdom of Alba.

860 AD Vikings invaded the northern and western isles. By this time the Scots had wised up to the "just looking for an ice-cream shop" ruse, but the Vikings had a new trick: "Where can we get a good fish supper?" The Scots were once again fooled and the Vikings took over the north and west.

870 AD Rampaging south, the Vikings stormed the Britons' capital at Dumbarton in revenge for the Britons beating them at beach volleyball.

890 AD The Vikings captured the Pictish fortress at Dunnottar, after the Picts went on holiday and forgot to lock the gates.

1116 AD One of the most famous of all Vikings was born in Scotland – Swein the Greatest. He was daring and dangerous, and liked to charge into battle wearing just his swimming trunks.

1263 AD The end of the Viking threat was nigh, after the Scots defeated the Vikings on the beachfront at the famous holiday resort of Largs. It was a hard battle: both sides excelled at air hockey and crazy golf; it was only the Scots' superior skill at playing the 2p slot machines that won the day.

1266 AD The Scots and Vikings signed the Treaty of Perth. The Vikings agreed to give the Hebrides and the Isle of Man to Scotland, as long as the Scots promised to STOP playing the bagpipes. The Scots agreed the Vikings could keep Orkney and Shetland, as long as they STOPPED attacking Scotland pretending they were just looking for seaside snacks.

1468 AD Cash-strapped Viking king Christian I pawned Orkney and Shetland to Scotland to pay for a new, exclusive, Viking-only beach resort. He soon realised he couldn't pay back the loan so the islands were given to Scotland permanently.

*These facts are mostly true, apart from the bit about the seaside.

Shetland

VIKINGS

Orkney

Hebrides

PICTS

Dunnottar

Iona

SCOTS

Dumbarton

Largs

BRITONS

ANGLES

Isle of Man

LITTLE KNOWN VIKING FACTS

Viking slaves were named after whatever job they did, for example Wilbur the Floor-Scrubber, Arnold the Barn-sweeper. The worst name to have was Cesspit-Cleaner.

Vikings used sheep's wool for wiping their bottoms. As far as we know the wool was sheered off the sheep first.

The most popular Viking games were called *Hnefatafl* and *Knattleikr*, the winner being anyone who could pronounce them.

Vikings brought all their cattle into the house in winter. As well as protecting animals from the cold it provided extra warmth for the house. Unfortunately nobody could sleep on account of all the loud cow farting.

Vikings lit fires with the help of human wee mixed with tree fungus.

CAN YOU SPOT 10 DIFFERENCES?

PERCY THE PIGEON POST

EST. 799AD   ODINSDAY 18th FEBRUARY   PRICE: ONE FRONT TOOTH

SKULL-SPLITTING NEWS

In what will forever be known as the **Awful Invasion** the Scots have narrowly missed being invaded by a band of maurauding Vikings, led by the fearsome Chief of Indgar, Harald the Skull-Splitter.

SPORTING HEADLINES

It is the weekend of the annual **Gruesome Games**. Word on the beach is that Thorfinn and his motley team have to save their village from the clutches of Magnus the Bone-Breaker. Odds are on for a new Chief of Indgar by Monday.

FOULSOME FOOD

It's all about Le Poisson (that's FISH to you boneheads). The King of Norway is on his way to Indgar and he expects a most **Disgusting Feast**. But there's a poisoner at large and the heat is on in the kitchen...

TORTUROUS TRAVEL

Early booking is essential to visit the **Rotten Scots'** most famous prisoner (that's Thorfinn) at Castle Red Wolf. Hurry – he may be rescued at any moment!

LOST AND NOT FOUND

A massive hoard of **Terrible Treasure** stolen from the pesky Scots has mysteriously vanished. Large reward promised for information leading to its recovery.

MISSING PERSONS

The **Raging Raiders** are prime suspects in the kidnapping of one harassed, goat-carrying Viking mum. Please report any sightings to Chief Harald the Skull-Splitter.

Collect all of Thorfinn's adventures!